First published in 1983 by Hodder and Stoughton
(Australia) Pty Limited
First American publication 1986 by Holiday House, Inc.
Printed in Hong Kong
© Michel and Sandra Laroche, 1983
Library of Congress Cataloging-in-Publication Data
Laroche, Michel.
    The snow rose.
    Summary: A troubador engages in a series of tests
to win the hand of a princess, but as time passes, he
realizes there is a prize more precious than the
cold-hearted princess.
    [1. Fairy tales] I. Laroche, Sandra, ill.
II. Title.
PZ8.L328Sn 1986   [E]   85-16391
ISBN 0-8234-0594-X

THE SNOW ROSE

To our parents and to Jesse

THE SNOW ROSE

Sandra & Michel Laroche

HOLIDAY HOUSE/NEW YORK

It was the time of the tales of yesteryear and a sudden spring downpour had soaked the long road through the Royal forest. A stranger, cold and wet to the skin, stopped his horse outside an inn. There would be a fire within by which he could warm and dry himself.

But the inn was filled with a jolly throng and he could not get near the welcoming fire which blazed merrily beneath a wide chimney. The stranger beckoned a serving girl and loudly ordered the best wine and a platter of bread and cheese to refresh his horse. When the people followed the girl, curious to see this wine-drinking animal, the cunning stranger moved close to the fire.

The innkeeper was soon hurrying back inside. "Sir," he said angrily. "You have made a fool of my daughter, Rose. Your beast will neither eat nor drink."

"Bring it all to me, then," grinned the stranger. The audience which crowded the doorway burst into merry laughter, but fell quiet when he added: "I need a good meal before I continue my journey to the castle, for I, Roland the Troubadour, have come to win the King's contest."

The innkeeper's shy daughter listened with interest. In spite of his brashness, she felt drawn to this handsome troubadour.

Spanning the river was a splendid Royal castle where the beautiful Princess Ermina lived with her father the King.

It was said that even the swans were not as graceful as Ermina. Each day, eager suitors from near and distant lands jostled in the antechambers to the Great Hall. But the vain Princess turned them all away, calling them fools and buffoons, not worth a snap of her charming fingers.

The old King desperately wanted to see his beloved daughter wed and he knew that only a very clever man could rule her heart. His search for a suitable husband had inspired the contest.

He offered, with the much-sought-after hand of the Princess, the prize of a third of his treasure. The latter he secured in an iron-bound chest, fastened with a knot so artfully conceived it would bewilder the craftiest of thieves. To undo the knot was the test.

The day of the contest was one of merrymaking. The vernal air resounded with the crowd's happy clamour and screams of delight, while above all sounded the shrill staccato of trumpets, calling the contestants to the court. Through all this pleasant confusion a long line of contestants wound towards the terrace where a dais had been built for the comfort of the King and his court.

Many nervous, yet nimble fingers tried in vain to undo the knot as the line of contestants slowly dwindled. And the beautiful Princess looked on with haughty disdain.

Dusk was falling when the troubadour arrived.

"Hello," a soft voice called from beneath the blossoming branches of an apple tree. It was Rose, the innkeeper's daughter, blushing as she spoke to the handsome troubadour.

He nonchalantly doffed his tricorne and confidently went on to join the line of contestants.

At last he climbed the steps to the dais and bowed low to the King. "Sire, is it not true that to win your daughter's hand I must undo the knot and open the chest?" The King nodded.

Unsheathing his sword Roland saluted the King. Then he turned to the chest, and, in one sweeping movement, slashed through the marvellous knot, saluted once more and returned his sword to its scabbard.

The chest at last stood free and the crowd cheered his audacity.

The King then held the troubadour's hand high above his head. "Both my treasures are now yours," he proclaimed before the excited crowd.

Hastily, Princess Ermina
tugged at the King's sleeve.
"Father," she said, "I know
that this man has succeeded,
but before he can be my
husband I think he should pass
a further test—he must be as
clever in summer as he has
been lucky in spring."

The King reluctantly agreed
and it was decided that Roland
would return during the feasts
of the summer solstice.
As the days warmed towards
summer, Roland and Rose were
often seen together by the
shady riverbanks, for they had
become friends. Whilst he
dreamed of melting the heart
of Princess Ermina, Rose would
shyly hold his hand and smile:
Neither noticed that, with a
surge of dark green, mid-
summer had arrived.

The eager troubadour presented himself before the King and his court on the terrace of the castle that spanned the river.

Before the hushed assembly the King pointed his cane at a huge egg atop a marble table. "Troubadour," he said, "if you can place this egg in such a way that it will stand on its smallest end, then you will win my daughter's hand."

A long moment passed while Roland considered the task. Then, with a glance towards the fair Princess, he took the egg and with a flourish, raised it. He then tapped it gently on the table, cracking the smallest end. The onlookers gasped, then murmured their admiration, for the egg was left standing as requested.

Jubilant, the old King placed a sure hand on the young man's shoulder and turned to his beloved daughter. She came swiftly to her father's side.

"Father," she cajoled sweetly, "I agree that this man has by a lucky hazard succeeded in passing this test. But before I accept him I must be sure that he will be as sharp-witted in autumn as he has been fortunate in summer."

Once again, because of his love for his daughter, the King agreed and announced to the disappointed crowd that Roland would return for a third contest at the time of the grape harvest festival.

Rose, the innkeeper's daughter quietly watched and smiled.

Summer faded and autumn
flooded the forest with colour.
The hearts of the innkeeper
and his wife were troubled, for
their daughter's shining eyes
could see no other than Roland
the troubadour—and he
scarcely knew she was there.
His eyes and heart were set on
a higher goal—the fair hand of
the Princess.

Mellow weeks passed until
that autumn day when the
grapes would run into new
wine. A radiant sun had risen
and the court was already
assembled in the Royal cellars
when Roland arrived for the
third contest.

To the gallant troubadour Ermina was even more beautiful than before and when her brilliant eyes flicked above her fan he caught her glance and held it for a fleeting moment.

The King rose to address the court. "Young man," he said, "this is the day of the third contest. Today you must bring me a newly-fallen star." The audience sighed in dismay.

Without a word Roland turned and made his way up curving flights of stairs, through the paved courtyard and across the drawbridge into the soft golden air of morning.

As the minutes grew into hours there was more and more shaking of heads as the court awaited Roland's return. The vaulted ceiling of the cellars echoed with Ermina's crystalline laughter.

Suddenly, Roland appeared, an apple held forth in his hand. A few nervous and amused giggles died when, halving the fruit sideways, he announced: "Look in the centre. Newly-fallen in your own orchard, Sire—a five-pointed star!"

All were well pleased and the crowd buzzed, but guileful Ermina again implored her father. "If I would take this man for my husband, then he must prove that his worthiness in winter equals his nimble wit in autumn."

So, Roland was to return on Christmas Eve. Loudly the onlookers voiced their disapproval, but Rose quietly smiled and Ermina's eyes sparkled mischievously above her fan.

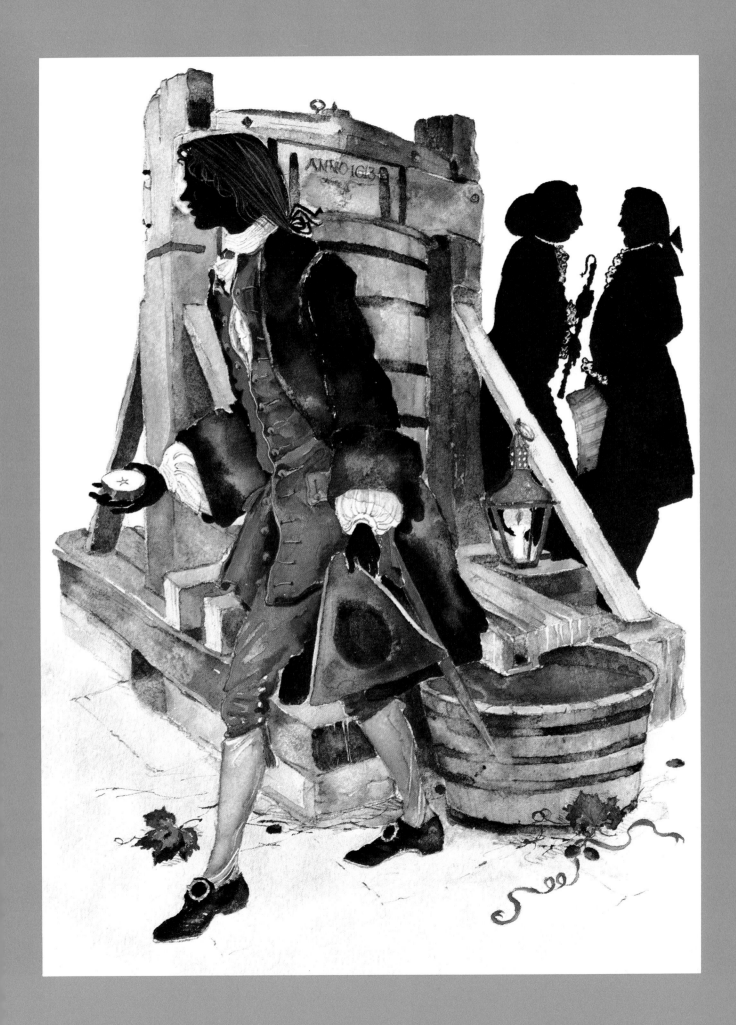

The arrival of winter brought heavy snow and Roland would take Rose with him on long sleigh rides. For the troubadour, time passed all too slowly but for Rose, December came much too soon, bringing a white, sleep-like stillness to everything as the land and river froze as one.

One morning bells rang from the castle that spanned the river. Wrapped in their warmest furs, the people gathered around glowing fires in the castle grounds. It was Christmas Eve and they would wait all day for Roland's return.

Ermina stood aloof at her father's side as Roland confidently approached the Royal assembly. A hush fell as she spoke.

"Troubadour!" Her sharp voice snapped out like an oiled whip. "Find me a flower, summersweet, as delicate and wild as those that rambled last June over the castle walls." She folded her small, white hands inside her muff and continued. "Bring it to me now and I will be yours."

Roland looked unflinchingly into her ice-blue eyes. All that could be heard was the crackling of the fires. At last he spoke.

"Princess, I have travelled, following the sun and sailed across the seven seas. I have seen the wealth of the Occident and the magnificence of the Orient. Yet only now, thanks to you, do I realize that there is no prize more precious than a summersweet flower, as delicate and wild as those that rambled last June over the castle walls. I have found my sweet wild flower, my flower for all seasons—my snow rose." He turned from the princess to the innkeeper's daughter.

The crowd went wild with joy and hats were thrown high in the star-strewn sky. As Rose blushed, Ermina's beautiful face paled. Shaking with jealousy and rage she gathered up the folds of her fur-trimmed cloak and fled.

On Christmas Day, Roland and Rose were wed and by Royal decree all the bells of the Kingdom joined together in one joyous carillon. Although he had not yet found a husband for his daughter, the King was pleased to bless this union. He had grown fond of the troubadour.

It is still remembered how the festivities went on until the New Year. Fires in the kitchens of the inn and the castle burned day and night, tables groaned with the weight of endless mouth-watering dishes, throats ached from singing and feet throbbed from dancing.

Never had there been a happier wedding or a merrier Christmas.